Nosy Tabitha Posy

written by
Julie Fulton

illustrated by
Jona Jung

Tabitha Posy was ever so nosy.
She made all her neighbours shout.
She'd peer round each door, ask, "Why?" and "What for?"
then pester them 'til she found out.

WANTED

Barney

"Please, leave us alone," they were all heard to moan,
but she grew even **worse** than before.
So they cried, "Get inside, draw the curtains and hide.
It's young Tabitha. Quick, lock your door!"

One day at her school, the new teacher, Miss Pool,
told the class, "We've got something to do.
It's a **bright** sunny day, so we'll all make our way
to see Hamilton Shady's new zoo."

Paint
PUZZLE
BLOCKS
ARITHMETIC
GEOGRAPHY 1

RED RAT SNAKE

They first saw a snake. It was called Wiggly Jake
and it slithered about in the trees.
All Tabitha said as it curled round her head was,
"Do you know if snakes ever sneeze?"

The owl gave a wail when she tugged at its tail.
It flew off with a shriek to its den.
"I just wanted to see if a feather would be
any good back at school as a pen."

OWL

DO NOT
FEED
THE BEAR

They went for a walk and heard noisy birds squawk.
They watched wallabies jumping around.
They saw penguins and bears, cheeky monkeys and hares,
and a tiger asleep on the ground.

It lay there and snored, so they all got quite bored
and decided to go off and play,
but young Tabitha said, "Look, the tiger's been fed.
What's he had for his dinner today?"

'DANGER!'

Miss Pool didn't see as she climbed up a tree,
but the tiger had opened an eye.
"Ooh, how nice; for a treat, I've been given fresh meat."
Grinned the tiger, "It's better than pie."

As Tabitha tried to creep up by its side,
the sly tiger began to look mean.

Then it swallowed her down without even a frown,
until only her legs could be seen.

Poor Tabitha cried as she jiggled inside
and the tiger began to feel sick.
It gave a loud moan, then a cough, then a groan,
but it only made Tabitha kick.

"I want to get out!" she said, wriggling about
with the feather she'd pinched from the owl.

It was tickly and so the poor tiger let go
and spat Tabitha up with a howl.

"Oh my!" said Miss Pool, "You are covered in drool
and there's spit dripping off your wet hair.
You've got mud on your dress and your face is a mess.
Can we get you cleaned up anywhere?"

An elephant's nose made a very good hose.
All the mud, spit and drool washed away.
As she stood there, wet through, soggy Tabitha knew
there was something she needed to say:

DO NOT PLAY THE TRUMPET!

Tabitha's Library
Sweet Spiders
YETI truth and myths
ELEPHANTS Questions without Answers
Screech Owls
Dark Side of the SUN
Winnie the Pooh
I LOVE SLIPPERY SNAKES
Astronomy
Under the Water
Architecture
Breeding Tigers
Alice in Wonderland
Dark Side of the Moon
Here and THERE
QUANTUM PHYSICS
TREASURES Guide for Hunters
What's hidden? in the mouse hole
I SPY at the ZOO
how to survive TROLLS
QUARKS for Advanced Students
DIGGING TUNNELS new guide
BEARS only for the brave
How To Train Your Dog
A secret Life of Earthworms
Exploring your granny's attic

"Please don't make a fuss. Let's get back on the bus.
I'm sorry," said Tabitha Posy.
"I think I should look for some things in a book,
rather than being too nosy."

The End